FIREMAN SAM

AND THE UNDERGROUND RESCUE

story by Rob Lee
illustrations by the County Studio

HEINEMANN · LONDON

Sarah and James were in Bella's cafe watching Bella pack a picnic hamper for them all.

"Yum yum!" drooled James, watching Bella pack jam sandwiches, fruit and crisps.

"And last but not least," said Bella triumphantly, "....a special chocolate cake – my favourite!"

When they saw Bella's treat, the twins couldn't wait.

Just then Bella's cat, Rosa, jumped up onto the table, almost knocking over a bottle of orangeade.

"Careful, Rosa!" cried Bella.

"Miaoow!" Rosa mewed as she rubbed against the hamper.

"I think she wants to come on the picnic, too, Bella," chuckled Sarah. Bella looked doubtful but the twins pleaded.

"Oh, alright," said Bella at last, wrapping up a small piece of fish for Rosa and shutting the hamper. "If we hurry we can catch Trevor's bus to Pandy Lane."

"I'll carry the hamper," said James.

"I thought you might," said Bella as they left the cafe.

In Dilys Price's shop, her son Norman was packing his
rucksack with fish hooks and bait tins.

"And where do you think you're going?" asked Dilys.

"Fishing, Mam," replied Norman.

"And who's going to help me in the shop, I'd like to know?"
asked Dilys.

"Aw, Mam," groaned Norman, taking a tin from his pocket.
"Have a sweet, Mam," he offered.

"You're Mummy's little darlin', aren't you?" cooed Dilys.
"Of course you can go fishing." She took a sweet and shrieked.
"YUK! It's a worm!" She dropped the wriggling worm and
Norman ran out of the shop laughing.

"NORMAN!" cried Dilys. But Norman was halfway to
Pandy Lane.

At the fire station, Penny Morris, from the Newtown brigade, was delivering a new supply of oxygen masks.

"You have a receiver and microphone in your mask," Penny explained, "so I can talk to you through this handset."

"Let's have a try," said Fireman Sam as he and Elvis put on the masks.

"Are you receiving me?" Penny spoke into the handset.

"Loud and clear!" replied Fireman Sam.

"Are you receiving me?" Penny asked Elvis. Elvis didn't reply. "Can you hear me?" Penny shouted into the receiver. Elvis took off his mask.

"Not much use these, Penny," he said. "All I can hear is Michael Jackson!"

"You're supposed to take your stereo off first!" sighed Fireman Sam.

"Oh, oh yeah," muttered Elvis, blushing.

Bella and the children had found a nice spot for their picnic.

"Ah, it's so peaceful here," sighed Bella as she unpacked the hamper.

"Except for the wasps," said Sarah, chasing one away.

"I don't know whether to have a jam sandwich first or the chocolate cake," said James.

"Just eat them both together," laughed Bella as she put Rosa's piece of fish on a plate.

Nobody had noticed Norman in the next field.

Norman hadn't noticed the picnickers either.

"I bet this river is packed with fish," he said as he busily baited his line. "Mam *will* be pleased when she sees all the fish I'll be taking home for tea."

Norman got ready to cast his line.

"Norman Price smashes the record: largest trout of the year caught in Pontypandy Pond!" he dreamt as he flicked the rod over his shoulder.

The line flew over the hedge behind Norman, towards the picnic party. Rosa looked up crossly as her fish was swept away from under her nose.

"My, you must have been hungry, Rosa," laughed Sarah. "You've cleaned your plate already!"

As Norman cast his line forward he was slapped on the back of his head by Rosa's fish.

"Strange," he muttered, "I'm catching fish on dry land!"

Curious, Norman peered over the hedge.

"Oooh! Bella's having a picnic," whispered Norman.

"Perhaps I should try a spot of jam buttie fishing for a change!"

Bella looked up in amazement as a jam sandwich flew up into the air.

"What on earth...?" she gulped.

"Great shot!" cried Norman, reeling in the sandwich. "Now for a slice of that chocolate cake!"

But the next time Norman was not so lucky. His rod hit a wasps' nest and a horde of angry wasps streamed out.

"Oh, no!" he cried as the wasps made straight for him. He jumped up and ran off across the field yelling "HELP! HELP!"

Norman ran as fast as he could until, finally, the wasps gave up.

"Phew!" he puffed as he stumbled through the deep grass. "I think I'm safe now."

Suddenly the ground gave way beneath him and he fell into a deep pit.

"Whooah!" Norman cried as he plunged downwards and landed with a bump. "It's d-dark in here," he stuttered, his voice echoing. "I'll never be able to climb back out, the sides are much too steep."

"Let's go for a walk," said Bella after they'd eaten. "Perhaps we can find my disappearing sandwich."

"I'll race you!" shouted James and he dashed off leaving Sarah behind.

"You started before me!" Sarah yelled back. "Watch out, Rosa! I'll trip over," she called as Rosa ran under her feet.

Looking over the hedge, James said, "Look! There's a rucksack."

"And a fishing rod," said Sarah, pointing further along the bank. "It looks like Norman's."

"I wonder where he is," said Bella.

"Come on, let's try and find him," said James.

When they came to the long grass Rosa pricked her ears.
"Do you hear something, Rosa?" asked Bella.
"I do!" cried James. "Listen!"
When they all stood quietly they heard a faint cry.
"Help! Help!"
Rosa dashed off.
"Quick! It's coming from over there!" called James,
running towards the hole.
"Help!" cried the voice again.
"It's Norman!" said Sarah.
They all peered into the dark hole.
"Don't go too near the edge," Bella warned.

"Are you alright, Norman?" Bella yelled down into the pit.

"I think so," replied Norman faintly. "But it's too steep for me to climb back out."

"Don't worry," Bella shouted back. "We'll get help. James, you'd better run to the phone box in Pandy Lane and call the fire brigade." James ran off as fast as he could.

Bella called to Norman.

"Stay where you are, Norman. Help is on the way."

At the fire station, Station Officer Steele ripped the message from the telex machine.

"What's up, Sir?" asked Fireman Sam.

"It's Norman Price," replied Station Officer Steele. "He's fallen into a pit near Pandy Lane!"

"It's probably that old disused mine shaft!" said Fireman Sam as they hurried towards Jupiter.

"Grab the oxygen masks, Cridlington," barked Station Officer Steele. "...At the double!"

"Yes, Sir!" replied Elvis, jumping to attention.

"I'll follow you, Sam!" shouted Penny Morris, leaping into the rescue tender.

The convoy sped through the streets of Pontypandy. Trevor Evans was just turning his bus into Pandy High Street when he heard the sirens. He braked sharply and pulled over to the side to let the engines go past.

"Blow me, they're in a hurry," he muttered, watching them speed off into the distance.

Meanwhile, down the pit, Norman was getting restless.

"Stay where you are," called Bella. "If you wander off you may get lost."

"I can hear Jupiter!" cried James.

Soon the two engines appeared over the hill.

"Don't worry," Sarah shouted to Norman, "Uncle Sam's on his way."

"He'll soon have you out safely," soothed Bella.

Meanwhile, unnoticed, Rosa had spotted a butterfly and darted off across the field after it.

The engines screeched to a halt near the pit and the crew piled out.

Fireman Sam lowered a gas detector into the hole and called down to Norman.

"Are you hurt, Norman?"

"I don't think so," Norman replied forlornly.

"There's no sign of gas down there, Sir," said Fireman Sam.

"You'd better take the masks just in case, Fireman Sam," replied Station Officer Steele.

"You'll need a spare one for Norman," said Penny.

Fireman Sam and Elvis checked their oxygen supply while Penny tested for radio contact.

"Are you receiving me?" she asked, speaking into the handset.

"Loud and clear!" replied Fireman Sam and Elvis as they lowered themselves down into the pit.

Norman was relieved when he saw Fireman Sam and Elvis coming down the mine shaft towards him.

"Don't worry," called Fireman Sam when he reached the bottom. "We'll soon have you out of here."

He shone his torch and could just make out Norman, crouching in a tunnel to one side of the pit.

"Watch your footing, Elvis. There are lots of loose rocks," Fireman Sam warned as he made his way towards Norman.

"Righto, Sam. Oh...Oops!" replied Elvis, tripping over a large stone.

"Are you alright, Elvis?" asked Fireman Sam.

"Nothing broken, thanks, Sam," sighed Elvis.

Just then they heard a slight rumble as one or two rocks fell from the roof at the mouth of the tunnel.

"Wh-what's that?" asked Elvis.

"You must have dislodged a beam," answered Fireman Sam as the rumble got louder.

Quickly Fireman Sam moved them all further up the tunnel to safety and seconds later the roof caved in, completely blocking the tunnel mouth.

"Great fires of London!" coughed Fireman Sam. "That was close!"

"We can't get back to the hole," said Elvis. "What do we do now?"

"Well, the first thing is for Norman to have one of these," said Fireman Sam, handing Norman an oxygen mask. "It's very dusty down here," he added as he fitted the mask on Norman.

Outside, at the edge of the hole, Station Officer Steele and Penny were waiting anxiously to hear what was going on when Bella suddenly realised that Rosa was missing.

"Where's that cat of mine now?" she wondered.

"Don't worry, Bella," said Sarah. "She'll come back when it's time for her tea."

But Rosa had chased the butterfly through the fields and into the wood before finally giving up. Tired of that game, she looked for something else to play at and trotted off to investigate an interesting-looking hole, half hidden by the bushes.

Inside the tunnel Fireman Sam called up Station Officer Steele on the intercom.

"There's too much rubble for us to move, Sir. We'll have to try and find another way out. There should be another entrance."

Fireman Sam, Elvis and Norman inched their way along the tunnel.

"Look, Fireman Sam, the tunnel forks," said Elvis peering through the gloom.

"Which way do we go?" asked Norman. Then suddenly they heard a "miaoow!"

Fireman Sam shone his torch down one of the tunnels.

"Look! There's Rosa!" he cried. "She didn't come in with us – there must be another way out."

Rosa scampered back down the tunnel into the darkness.

"Quick!" said Fireman Sam. "Let's follow her." And the three of them hurried down the tunnel after Rosa.

"Now where's she gone?" Norman asked.

"Miaow!" called Rosa again.

"There she is," said Norman, catching sight of her eyes shining in the dark.

"There!" cried Elvis, watching Rosa squeeze between the boards across the exit. "Rosa's saved us!"

But when they arrived at the boarded-up entrance Fireman Sam looked disappointed.

"Not so fast, Elvis," he said. "We'll never get through that gap and these boards are nailed up solid."

Meanwhile Rosa had scampered off across the fields.

Station Officer Steele was just about to contact the firemen on the radio when he heard a "miaow" behind him.

"My Rosa's come back," cried Bella, running forward to pick up her cat. But Rosa dashed off again before Bella could catch her.

"I think she wants us to follow her!" said Bella excitedly.

"Perhaps she knows where Uncle Sam is," said Sarah.

"Right!" ordered Station Officer Steele, taking command. "Follow that cat!"

Rosa ran across the fields with Bella, Sarah and James hot on her heels. Penny and Station Officer Steele followed in the two engines, racing over the bumpy ground.

"I hope Rosa's not taking us butterfly chasing," puffed Bella.

"Or wild goose chasing!" added Sarah.

"No," cried James, "I think Rosa's found the entrance to the mine."

The engines screeched to a halt at the entrance and Station Officer Steele jumped down.

"Anyone hurt?" he enquired briskly, peering through the gap in the boards.

"No, Sir. We're right as rain," replied Sam. "Or at least we will be when we get out of here."

"I'll have you out in no time," smiled Penny as she took a chainsaw from the locker of her rescue tender. "This should do the trick."

Penny pulled the cord and the saw roared into life.
"Stand well back," she called.

Inside, Fireman Sam, Elvis and Norman covered their ears
as Penny quickly sawed through the wood. Sawdust flew
everywhere and in no time the entrance was clear.

"Very efficient, I must say, Penny," said Fireman Sam
admiringly as they all stepped out into the sunlight.

Everybody piled into the vehicles and they drove off
towards Pontypandy.

"You've been very brave, Norman," said Station Officer
Steele, "so just this once we'll use the sirens."

Norman beamed with excitement. "I should fall down mine
shafts more often," he thought to himself.

The sirens were still blaring when they pulled up outside
his mum's shop.

"Am I on fire?" asked Dilys, running outside.

Fireman Sam laughed and explained what had happened.

"But don't worry, Dilys," he soothed. "There's no harm
done."

"Mummy's brave little boy," cooed Dilys, smothering
Norman with hugs and kisses.

"Aw, Mam!"

Later that day, Fireman Sam and the crew were relaxing at Bella's when Norman appeared at the door carrying a plate of fish wrapped in a big bow.

"This is for Rosa, for fishing us out of the mine!" said Norman shyly.

"I'll second that," cheered Fireman Sam. "Congratulations, Firefighter Rosa!"

FIREMAN SAM SAYS:

There's lots to do in the countryside, but always remember to tell someone where you're going before you set out alone.

First published 1990 by William Heinemann Ltd
an imprint of Reed Consumer Books Limited
Michelin House, 81 Fulham Road, London SW3 6RB
and Auckland, Melbourne, Singapore and Toronto
Reprinted 1991, 1992
Fireman Sam copyright © 1985 Prism Art & Design Ltd
Text copyright © 1990 Reed International Books Limited
Illustrations copyright © 1990 Reed International Books Limited
All rights reserved
Based on the animation series produced by
Bumper Films for S4C – Channel 4 Wales –
and Prism Art & Design Ltd
Original idea by Dave Gingell and Dave Jones,
assisted by Mike Young
Characters created by Rob Lee
ISBN 0 434 97337 8
Printed in Italy by OFSA - Milano